I0606278
STAND-UP PADDLEBOARDING
OUTDOOR ADVENTURES and SPORTS
Katie Gillespie
AV2
www.openlightbox.com

Step 1
Go to **www.openlightbox.com**

Step 2
Enter this unique code
SDPBMHCKB

Step 3
Explore your interactive eBook!

AV2 is optimized for use on any device

Your interactive eBook comes with...

Contents
Browse a live contents page to easily navigate through resources

Audio
Listen to sections of the book read aloud

Videos
Watch informative video clips

Weblinks
Gain additional information for research

Slideshows
View images and captions

Try This!
Complete activities and hands-on experiments

Key Words
Study vocabulary, and complete a matching word activity

Quizzes
Test your knowledge

Share
Share titles within your Learning Management System (LMS) or Library Circulation System

Citation
Create bibliographical references following the Chicago Manual of Style

This title is part of our AV2 digital subscription

1-Year K–5 Subscription
ISBN 978-1-7911-3320-7

Access hundreds of AV2 titles with our digital subscription.
Sign up for a FREE trial at **www.openlightbox.com/trial**

OUTDOOR ADVENTURES and SPORTS

STAND-UP PADDLEBOARDING

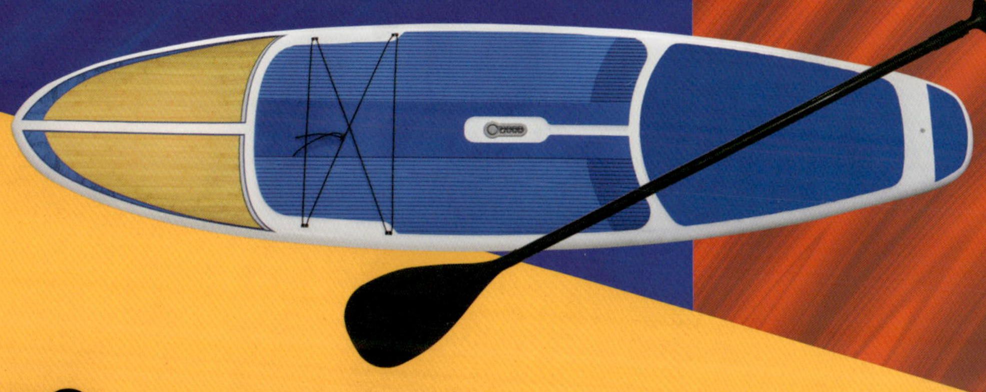

CONTENTS

All About Stand-Up Paddleboarding

Stand-up paddleboarding is a water sport that is often referred to as SUP. As the name suggests, it involves a paddle and a board. Participants ride on the board. They use a long paddle to propel it across the water.

Fishers in Peru are widely believed to have been the first to perform a version of SUP. As early as 1000 BC, they used 12-foot (4-meter) watercraft made of reeds. The fishermen would stand up on the vessels, using a shaft of bamboo to paddle. Sometimes, after the day's fishing was done, they would continue riding the vessels across the water for fun.

Over the years, other forms of SUP appeared, notably in Israel and Italy. However, it was not until the 1900s that the sport known today started to form. Originating in Hawaii, modern SUP is typically attributed to a group of surfing instructors known as the Waikiki Beach Boys. While teaching, they would stand on their surfboards and steer with paddles in order to better see their students. By the early 2000s, SUP had spread to California, where racing contests helped the sport grow in popularity. Today, SUP has millions of fans across the globe.

Changes Throughout the Years

PAST	PRESENT
People stood on watercraft to catch fish or transport objects.	People all over the world practice SUP for recreation, exercise, or as a competitive sport.
Vessels were made of tightly bundled reeds.	Paddleboards are made of materials such as fiberglass, foam, and plastic.
Bamboo shafts were used for paddling.	Paddles are made of a variety of materials. They come with different blade shapes and sizes.
Watercraft were usually quite unstable.	Riders can choose the right board to properly support their height and weight.

Getting Started

SUP beginners often start out by cruising. This type of recreational paddling is fairly easy, covering short distances at a relaxed pace. Touring SUP covers longer distances. It is more physically demanding than recreational paddling.

Some people enjoy fishing from their paddleboards, since standing up allows them to see far under water. Others want a more thrilling paddling experience. They may try surfing SUP, which is often done on ocean waves, or **whitewater** SUP, which takes place on **rapids.** Competitive paddlers can try SUP racing. This kind of SUP uses longer boards that are designed for speed.

No matter which form of SUP paddlers are interested in, they need to have the proper gear. The right equipment can help keep paddlers safe. Paddlers must also know how to use it if something goes wrong.

1 One of the main pieces of equipment needed for SUP is the board. Boards come in a variety of shapes and sizes. Some SUP boards are hard, while others are **inflatable.**

2 Paddlers use paddles to control where the board goes. Some paddles are a fixed length, while others are **adjustable.**

3 A personal flotation device (PFD), such as a life jacket, is an important piece of safety gear. It will keep a paddler afloat if he or she falls into the water. It also makes it easier for the paddler to climb back onto the board.

Different forms of SUP may require particular skills, shapes or sizes of boards, or water conditions.

4 Worn around the ankle or waist, a leash secures the board to the paddler. This prevents the board and paddler from getting separated if the paddler falls into the water. Leashes can be straight or coiled.

5 Paddlers should wear waterproof clothing and dress appropriately for the weather and season. In cold air and water conditions, a **wetsuit** can help prevent **hypothermia**.

6 A dry bag is a waterproof container. It can hold essential items that may be useful in an emergency, such as a first-aid kit, cell phone, or change of clothes.

Stand-Up Paddleboarding Basics

Paddlers must learn to mount and launch their boards. They should secure their leash when they first reach the shore. Then, they can carry the board into shallow water. Despite the sport's name, not all of SUP is done while standing up. Paddlers should mount the board on their knees before moving away from the shore.

It can be tricky to stand up on a paddleboard. Going from a kneeling to a standing position should be done slowly and gradually. Paddlers start by moving into a squat and then pushing up with their legs. Once they are standing, the paddle can be inserted into the water. This helps provide balance.

While many boards are designed for a single rider, some can hold another person or even a dog as a passenger.

Some people incorrectly hold their paddle like a broomstick, with both hands on the shaft, or handle. The proper way to hold the paddle is by gripping the top with one hand and holding the center of the shaft with the other hand. The blade, which is the end of the paddle, should be angled toward the front of the board. There are many possible **strokes**, but beginners should at least be familiar with the three basic ones. The forward stroke propels the board ahead. The reverse stroke is used to slow down or stop. The sweep stroke causes the board to turn left or right.

Unlike traditional surfing, which requires waves, SUP can be done in a variety of conditions. People can SUP on almost any flat or rough body of water. This means that lakes, rivers, oceans, and even large swimming pools are all potential SUP spots.

Most boards have a carry handle in the middle. This makes them easier to carry into and out of the water.

Stand-Up Paddleboarding Levels

People of all ages and fitness levels can participate in SUP, adding to its widespread appeal. However, this does not mean that potential paddlers can jump straight into the water without any training. Beginners should take lessons to learn the basics.

Skills courses designed for new students provide an introduction to SUP and teach the essentials. Students learn about safety and equipment. They also increase their paddling abilities by developing and improving their skills in different conditions. Students may practice paddling in the presence of waves, **currents**, and wind. Higher-level skills courses are available as well.

After the successful completion of their skills courses, students can move on to skills assessments. These courses provide a progression in skill development. They test students on their SUP knowledge and experience.

Higher-level skills courses often cover specific topics, such as river, whitewater, ocean, and coastal SUP.

For those who are interested in continuing their paddling education and teaching others, the next step is to take an instructor certification course. In addition to teaching paddling knowledge and techniques, these courses focus on group management, judgment, and teaching strategies. Once certified as instructors, paddlers can work toward endorsements. These specialized courses allow SUP instructors to teach skills that are not part of the traditional instructor workshops.

Paddlers can take courses on how to safely perform SUP yoga.

Levels of SUP Courses

- SKILLS COURSES — Step 1
- SKILLS ASSESSMENTS — Step 2
- INSTRUCTOR CERTIFICATES — Step 3
- ENDORSEMENTS — Step 4

Staying Safe

Although SUP is a fun activity, it does come with some risks. One of the biggest concerns is a sudden change in the weather. Paddlers should always check the weather forecast before a SUP journey. They must be aware of any potential hazards, such as wind or fog. If paddlers hear thunder or see lightning during a SUP session, they should get back to shore immediately. It is not safe to be on the water during a storm.

Paddlers need to pay attention to their surroundings. Depending on the body of water, they may have to watch for currents or waves. Sharp rocks can be a concern as well, along with motorboats or other water vehicles. Beginners should start on calmer water and stay close to shore. For added safety, they can paddle with a partner.

The rules for SUP can vary between states or countries. It is the responsibility of paddlers to know and comply with all rules for their area. Specific types of equipment may be required after dark, in certain locations, or for younger participants. Required equipment often includes safety gear, such as a PFD, leash, waterproof flashlight, whistle, or **compass**. Other items, such as a **license**, may be necessary as well.

Common Paddleboard Shapes

All Round

Wave

Touring

Race

#1 Paddling Tip

It is always a good idea to have a trip plan. Before your SUP journey, tell someone onshore where you will be going and when you expect to return.

In some places, a SUP board is considered a watercraft. This means there could be additional rules to follow. For instance, SUP boards might need to remain a certain distance from the shore.

Explore the Outdoors

There are several outdoor adventures similar to SUP that can be enjoyed on the water. Some of these are surfing, wakeboarding, kiteboarding, and sailboarding.

Surfing

Surfing is one of the world's most popular water sports. As in SUP, surfers use a board to get on top of the water. However, surfboards are shorter, narrower, lighter, and thinner than SUP boards. They have a similar shape, but a greater curve. Surfers do not use a paddle. Instead, they lie on their stomachs and paddle with their hands. The main goal of surfing is to stand up and ride an unbroken wave toward the shore.

Wakeboarding

Wakeboarding is a combination of surfing, water skiing, and snowboarding. It was invented in the 1980s. Today, millions of people wakeboard worldwide. Participants stand on a board and ride it across the water. Instead of paddling, wakeboarders are towed by an overhead cable or behind a boat, at speeds of about 30 miles (48 kilometers) per hour. Riders wear boots called bindings that fasten to their boards, which are long and curved.

Kiteboarding

In kiteboarding, participants stand on a twin tip board. The board is attached to the rider's feet. A large, hand-controlled kite pulls the rider across the water. Powered by the wind and steered with a control bar, this kite is connected to a harness worn around the rider's waist. When the kite catches the wind, riders can jump or perform other stunts. Kiteboarding is an exciting activity that requires plenty of open space. It is usually done on oceans or large lakes.

Sailboarding

Also called windsurfing, sailboarding combines surfing with sailing. Participants ride on a craft called a sailboard, which is a board rigged with a sail. The size of the board and sail can vary, depending on the type of sailing, wind conditions, and the skill level of the rider. Unlike surfing, sailboarding can be done anywhere there is water and wind.

Stand-Up Paddleboarding Around the World

There are countless places to go stand-up paddleboarding. Some paddlers choose locations for their natural beauty and scenic views. Others prefer to visit destinations with rich histories and cultures. The following are some of the most popular and spectacular SUP sites in the world.

1 Hawaii, United States

The birthplace of modern SUP, Hawaii is one of the sport's most popular destinations. On the north shore of the island of Oahu, paddlers can see coral reefs and may even spot whales.

2 Lake Tahoe, United States

With a 72-mile (116-km) shoreline, Lake Tahoe is the largest **alpine** lake in North America. Lake Tahoe's crystal clear water and photogenic mountain backdrop make it an ideal SUP spot for beginners.

3 Bali, Indonesia

Known for its ancient temples and lush vegetation, Bali is a stunning place. Featuring different types of waves, Bali's coasts are perfect for paddlers of all skill levels.

4 Amsterdam, Netherlands

Amsterdam is home to 165 canals, which offer a unique perspective of the city's beautiful architecture. Paddlers can explore on their own or take a guided tour to learn about Amsterdam's many historical buildings and landmarks.

Join the Club

There are several organizations related to SUP. One of the oldest and most important is the American Canoe Association (ACA). It supports paddleboarding, canoeing, rafting, and other paddle sports by educating paddlers and organizing competitions. Founded in the United States in 1880, the ACA now has members in many countries.

Another well-known organization is the World Paddle Association (WPA). It was started in 2010 by a pair of paddling enthusiasts and focuses specifically on SUP. The WPA's main goal is to provide a global standard for competitive SUP events. It is highly respected in the SUP community as it is run by current and former professional stand-up paddleboarders. The WPA also works with an organization called the Association of Paddlesurf Professionals (APP) to arrange SUP races.

In addition to being a popular recreational activity, SUP is also a professional sport. There are many competitions around the world. These include distance races and sprints.

There is a strong push for SUP to be included in the Olympic Games. In 2020, it was decided that, if SUP becomes an Olympic sport, the International Surfing Association (ISA) will be responsible for making the arrangements. It is possible that SUP could be part of the 2028 Olympics.

The ACA provides educational programs that reach more than 800,000 people each year.

The APP World Tour is one of the largest SUP races in the world. This exciting international series takes place across multiple different countries each year.

Healthy Habits

Paddlers need proper nutrition before, during, and after a SUP session. Eating a meal about one hour ahead of time is recommended. It should include healthy fats and proteins. Scrambled eggs and whole grain toast or chicken salad with vegetables are good options. Portable snacks, such as nuts, dried fruit, and beef jerky, can be brought along on the water.

In order to perform at their best, paddlers must also drink plenty of water. This will decrease the risk of **dehydration**, which can cause cramps, weakness, or other more severe conditions. To stay hydrated while on a SUP journey, paddlers can bring a reusable water bottle. Hands-free hydration backpacks are also a popular choice.

SUP is a full-body workout. It takes strong legs and upper body muscles to stay standing on the board.

Paddling uses back, arm, and shoulder muscles. It is a low-impact activity that offers many fitness benefits. In addition to building strength and improving balance, SUP is also great for **cardiovascular** health.

Grip strength is crucial for SUP. Paddlers must be able to maintain a good grip on the paddle throughout each SUP journey. Forearm fatigue and hand cramps are common problems. To ensure that their hands do not become too tired or sore to paddle, paddlers should build up their grip strength and endurance. A simple exercise such as repeatedly squeezing a tennis ball can help paddlers develop their hand muscles and increase stamina.

Always make sure your paddle grip is shoulder width apart. If your grip is too short, there will not be enough power behind your strokes.

Tennis Ball Squeeze

1. Hold a tennis ball in one hand.
2. Squeeze the ball and hold for two seconds.
3. Relax your grip on the ball. Repeat 5 to 15 times.
4. Rest for one minute.
5. Do two more sets with the same hand.
6. Switch hands and repeat the exercise.

Quiz

1. What should paddlers do if there is a storm?
2. Why should paddlers wear a leash?
3. How can paddlers stay hydrated on the water?
4. Who were the first people to perform a version of SUP?
5. What is the proper way to hold the paddle?
6. Which is the largest alpine lake in North America?

Answers

1. If thunder or lightning occurs during a SUP session, paddlers should get back to shore immediately. **2.** A leash secures the board to the paddler and prevents the board and paddler from getting separated if the paddler falls into the water. **3.** To stay hydrated while on a SUP journey, paddlers can bring a reusable water bottle. Hands-free hydration backpacks are also a popular choice. **4.** Peruvian fishermen stood up to ride crafts across the water as early as 1000 BC. **5.** The proper way to hold the paddle is by gripping the top with one hand and holding the center of the shaft with the other hand. The blade should be angled toward the front of the board. **6.** With a 72-mile (116-km) shoreline, Lake Tahoe is the largest alpine lake in North America.

Key Words

adjustable: able to be changed to different sizes
alpine: relating to mountains
cardiovascular: relating to the heart and blood vessels
compass: a tool that uses a magnetic needle to determine direction
currents: the flows and movements of water in a certain direction
dehydration: when the body does not have enough water
hypothermia: a dangerous loss of body heat caused by extremely cold weather
inflatable: able to be filled with air or gas
license: an official document that gives permission to do something
rapids: shallow parts of rivers where rocks are exposed and fast-moving water creates waves
strokes: repeated movements that propel a person or vessel in a particular direction in the water
wetsuit: a close fitting rubber suit worn to retain body heat in cold water
whitewater: very strong, fast-moving water, often found in rivers

Index

Get the best of both worlds.

AV2 bridges the gap between print and digital.

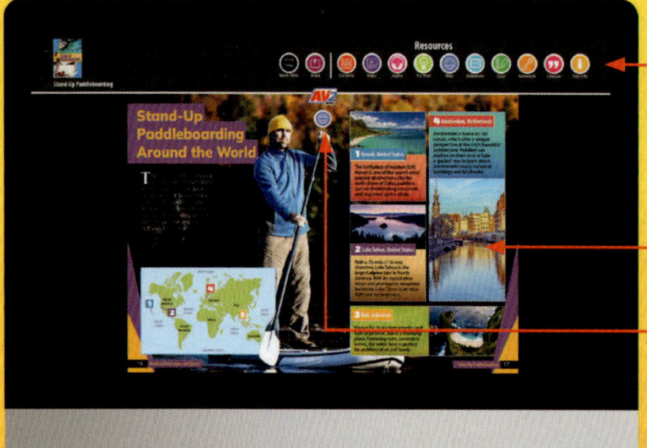

The expandable resources toolbar enables quick access to content including **videos**, **audio**, **activities**, **weblinks**, **slideshows**, **quizzes**, and **key words**.

Animated videos make static images come alive.

Resource icons on each page help readers to further **explore key concepts**.

Published by Lightbox Learning Inc.
276 5th Avenue, Suite 704 #917
New York, NY 10001
Website: www.openlightbox.com

Library of Congress Cataloging-in-Publication Data

Names: Gillespie, Katie, author.
Title: Stand-up paddleboarding / Katie Gillespie.
Description: New York, NY : Lightbox Learning Inc., 2023. | Series: Outdoor adventures and sports | Includes index. | Audience: Grades 4-6
Identifiers: LCCN 2022024088 (print) | LCCN 2022024089 (ebook) | ISBN 9781791147518 (library binding) | ISBN 9781791147525 (paperback) | ISBN 9781791147532
Subjects: LCSH: Stand-up paddle surfing--Juvenile literature.
Classification: LCC GV840.S68 G55 223 (print) | LCC GV840.S68 (ebook) | DDC 797.3/2--dc23/eng/20220604
LC record available at https://lccn.loc.gov/2022024088
LC ebook record available at https://lccn.loc.gov/2022024089

Printed in Guangzhou, China
1 2 3 4 5 6 7 8 9 0 26 25 24 23 22

082022
101121

Project Coordinator Priyanka Das
Designer Terry Paulhus

Photo Credits
Every reasonable effort has been made to trace ownership and to obtain permission to reprint copyright material. The publisher would be pleased to have any errors or omissions brought to its attention so that they may be corrected in subsequent printings. The publisher acknowledges Alamy, Bridgeman Images, Getty Images, and Shutterstock as its primary image suppliers for this title.